bitty ⭐ baby
the brave

by Kirby Larson
& Sue Cornelison

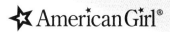

⭐ American Girl®

Special thanks to Dr. Laurie Zelinger, consultant,
child psychologist, and registered play therapist.
Dr. Zelinger reviewed and helped shape the "For Parents"
section, which was written by editorial staff.

Published by American Girl Publishing

Questions or comments? Call 1-800-845-0005,
visit **americangirl.com,** or write to Customer Service,
American Girl, 8400 Fairway Place, Middleton, WI 53562-0497.

Printed in China
13 14 15 16 17 18 19 20 LEO 10 9 8 7 6 5 4 3 2

Series Editorial Development: Jennifer Hirsch & Elizabeth Ansfield
Art Direction and Design: Susan Walsh & Gretchen Becker
Production: Tami Kepler, Judith Lary, Paula Moon, Kristi Tabrizi

For Mary the Brave
K.L.

For my sons, Bryce and Garrett
S.C.

Bitty Baby and I were going for a sleepover
at Grammy and Grampa's new house.
Our dog Winston was coming, too.

Bitty Baby and I packed our pink
pajamas and a flashlight and
our Go Fish cards
in our sleepover
suitcase.

"Will we like the new house?" I asked Mommy.

"You will," she said. "Because Grammy and Grampa are there."

At Grammy and Grampa's new house, some
things were still the same. Like the cookie jar
for the cookies Grampa bakes. And the china
cups for tea parties with Grammy.

And a big-girl bed for Bitty Baby and me.

But one thing was not the same. Grammy and Grampa's new house had a basement!

I wanted to go downstairs to play right away. "Grammy said we could use all the blankets and cushions to build a fort," I said. "And Grampa gave us some cookies for a snack."

"It's a long way down," said Bitty Baby.

"How about if I hold your hand?" I asked.

"And I can hold yours," said Bitty Baby.

We walked down, down, down the stairs.

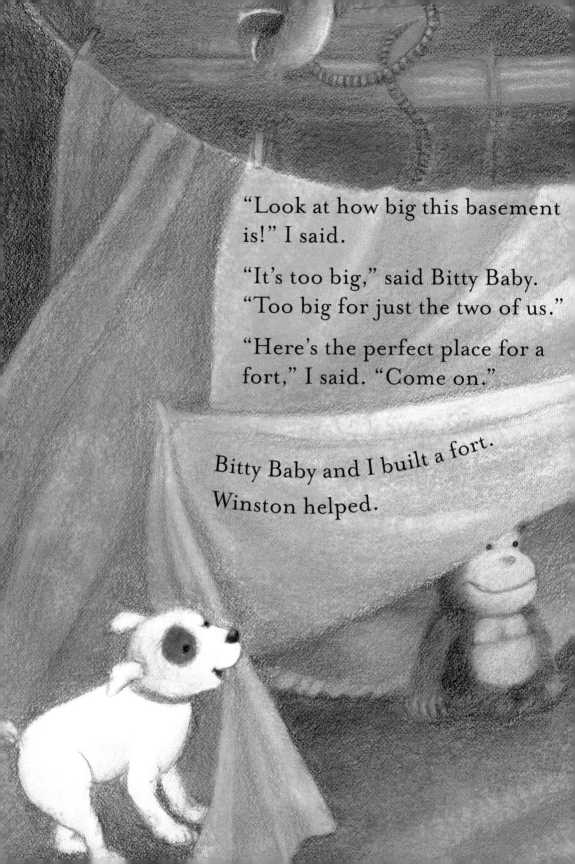

"Look at how big this basement is!" I said.

"It's too big," said Bitty Baby. "Too big for just the two of us."

"Here's the perfect place for a fort," I said. "Come on."

Bitty Baby and I built a fort. Winston helped.

We climbed inside.
"Isn't Grammy and Grampa's
new house fun?" I asked.

"Their old house wasn't so dark," said Bitty Baby.

I turned on the flashlight. "Now it's not so dark. Wou
you like a cookie?" Bitty Baby wanted one for each ha

Then we heard a noise. A **grumbly**, **gurgly** noise.

"What's that?" asked Bitty Baby.

"It's coming from over there," I said. "Let's not think about it. Do you want to play Go Fish?"

Bitty Baby shook her head. "This fort is dark. And full of funny noises." She looked scared.

"Shall I tell a loud story?" I asked. "So we don't hear the noises?"

Bitty Baby nodded. "A very loud story."

We all snuggled together.

"Once upon a time, Bitty Baby put three cookies, a flashlight, and some Go Fish cards into her purse. Then she went for a walk in the jungle.

She hadn't gone very far when she met a giant gorilla. He waved his arms. He beat his chest. He showed his teeth.

"What's wrong?" Bitty Baby asked.
She could speak Gorilla.

"I heard a scary noise," said Gorilla.
"A **grumbly**, **gurgly** noise."

Bitty Baby knew what to do. She opened her purse. "Would you like a cookie?" she asked.

"A cookie is a very good idea," said Gorilla. "Thank you."

He was so polite, Bitty Baby gave him two cookies—one for each hand.

"Good-bye," she said.

"Don't go!" said Gorilla. "I'm scared to stay by myself!"

"Well then," said Bitty Baby, "you'd better come with me."

Deeper into the dark, dark jungle they went.
One of the thick vines above their heads moved.

It was no vine—it was a giant boa constrictor!
He was headed right for Bitty Baby and Gorilla.

"What's wrong?" asked Bitty Baby. She could
speak Boa Constrictor.

"I heard an awful noise," said Boa.
"A **grumbly**, **gurgly** noise.
But it's too dark to see where
it was coming from."

Bitty Baby knew what to do.
She opened her purse.

"How about a
flashlight?" she aske
She knew that even
the biggest boas are
sometimes afraid of
the dark.

A flashlight is a very good idea," said Boa.

Here, you can keep it," said Bitty Baby.
Good-bye!" Bitty Baby and Gorilla started off.

Don't go!" said Boa. "I'm scared to stay by myself."

Well then," said Bitty Baby, "you'd better come
with us."

Bitty Baby and Gorilla and
Boa kept going. Then they
heard an awful noise.

A **grumbly** noise.

A **gurgly** noise.

Gorilla and Boa hid.
Bitty Baby peeked
around a tree.

They saw a giant
elephant!

"Who's there?"
Elephant trumpeted.

Gorilla
and Boa
trembled.

"Were you crying just now?" Bitty Baby asked
bravely. She could speak Elephant.

"Not me." Elephant blew his trunk on a very big hanky.

"We heard a **grumbly, gurgly** noise. A noise like an elephant crying," said Bitty Baby.

Elephant's head drooped. "I might have been crying a little," he said. "It's scary being in the jungle by myself. It's dark, and there are funny noises."

"The jungle's not so scary," said Gorilla.

"Not anymore," said Boa.

"That's right," said Bitty Baby. "The jungle is not so scary with friends."

Then she taught Gorilla, Boa, and Elephant how to play Go Fish. Everyone won a game.

"It's time for me to go home,"
said Bitty Baby. Her new
friends cried a little.

Not because they were
afraid, but because
they were sad that she
was leaving.

Bitty Baby hugged
them good-bye and
promised to come
back and visit. Very
soon. The end.

"I like that story," said Bitty Baby. "And I like being here with you. But this basement is still too big for the two of us."

"Not for long," I said. "I have a good idea!"

Grammy and Grampa thought it was a good idea, too.

For Parents

Traveling with Children

Although children feel most comfortable in familiar surroundings, they are extremely adaptable and love exploring new places. They thrive on knowing what's next, so when you're traveling, prepare them for the changes they'll experience.

Before You Go

Talk about the upcoming trip: where you're going, how you'll get there, who will be there with you, and the exciting things you'll do when you arrive. If you're visiting relatives or old family friends, show your daughter pictures of them so that they will seem familiar to her when she gets there. (After all,

if she hasn't seen the people in a while, they may seem like strangers to her now.)

Describe what you will need for the trip, and let your little one help you pack. Help her choose a few comfort items, such as a favorite stuffed animal or toys, some books, and a blankie.

If the trip means your girl will be apart from people she usually sees every day, such as siblings, a parent or a regular caregiver, let her know. Consider bringing along a picture of "left behind" family members for her to look at when she misses them.

Once You Arrive

Walk around and explore together to help your daughter become familiar and feel comfortable in her new surroundings. If she's shy with new people, that's very common. Don't expect her to feel at ease right away with people she has never met or hasn't seen in a while. Give her time to relax and warm up.

Show her where she can eat, sleep, and play. If any areas are off-limits, let her know, and explain the limitations. Having some familiar foods available will help her feel more at home in the new place.

If you will be leaving your little one alone with her hosts, tell her when she will see you again. If possible, make a plan to call and say good night so that she can look forward to hearing your voice before she goes to sleep.

Remember to prepare yourself for the trip, too! Your child can sense when you are stressed or uneasy. If you seem relaxed and happy to be taking a trip and visiting a new place, she will be, too.

For more parent tips, visit **americangirl.com/BittyParents**

loving

curious

confident